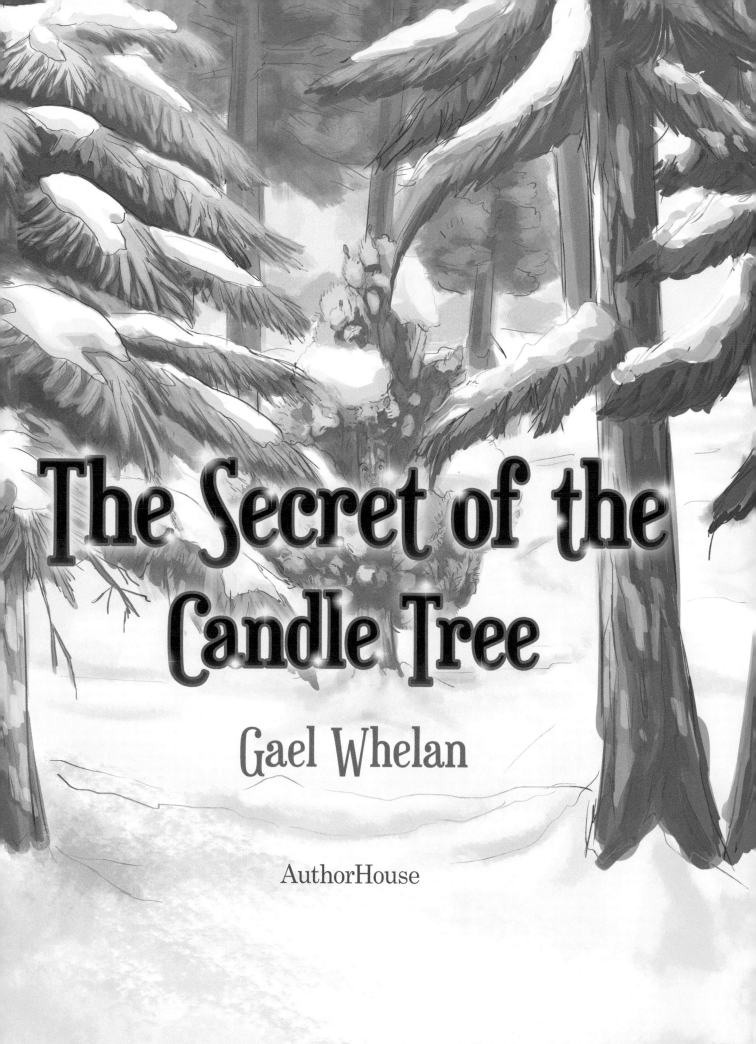

The Secret of the Candle Tree

Gael Whelan

AuthorHouse

AuthorHouse™ UK
1663 Liberty Drive
Bloomington, IN 47403 USA
www.authorhouse.co.uk
Phone: 0800 047 8203 (Domestic TFN)
+44 1908 723714 (International)

This book is printed on acid-free paper.

ISBN: 978-1-7283-9497-8 (sc)
ISBN: 978-1-7283-9496-1 (e)

Print information available on the last page.

Published by AuthorHouse 11/12/2019

authorHOUSE®

This book was written for my dear nephew Nathaniel
and is dedicated to Dr Lyle Grant

Eight-year old Nathaniel was singing as he entered the house:

"Angels from the realms of Glory
Wing your way o'er all the earth.
Ye who sang creation's story,
Now proclaim the Messiah's birth.
Glooooooria in excelsis Deo!
Glooooooria in excelsis Deo!"

"Mom?" he called.

"Mom?" he called. "Mum, are you home?"

"I'm here," replied his mother.

Nathaniel followed the sound of her voice to the kitchen. "Gee, Mom, those cookies smell good. Please, may I have one?"

"You may have one gingerbread cookie; the rest are for the Nativity concert tonight. How was the final rehearsal?"

"Fine, but I look dumb dressed up as a tree. Why can't I be an angel, or one of the wise men who come on the camels to find the baby? All the other characters have a gift to give to the new baby, but what can a tree give?"

"Every member of the cast is important to the story of the birth of that special baby, Nathaniel, even the tree."

"You keep telling me that, Mom. But how does a funny tree with skinny cones on it get to be important?"

"Well, my boy, the actual night that the baby was to be born was—"

"I know, over two thousand years ago. But it doesn't say why the tree became important," chimed in Nathaniel. "I mean, how do you know that this kind of tree grew near Bethlehem?"

"Nathaniel, I was going to tell you the legend of the Candle Tree later tonight, before the concert, but I think you need to hear it now." While he ate his gingerbread cookie and drank a cup of hot chocolate, his mother began the tale.

"The night that the little baby was to be born in Bethlehem, the angels in heaven were very excited; the Creator had given them permission to fly around the earth, to tell all the people of the world about the coming birth of the baby.

"They set off towards earth, and were soon flying across the enormous forests of the country we now know as Canada. The angels didn't know, however, that the aurora borealis had also heard the news of the impending birth of this special boy. Its shimmering lights danced across the sky in brilliant red, green, and white layers. Perhaps it was the exceptional brightness of the aurora borealis which woke the tree from his winter nap, or it may have been the old elk who rubbed itself against the tree.

The tree stretched out a couple of his branches and wiggled his pinecones, then looked around to see why spring had arrived in the forest, at night. He gazed up in wonder at the northern lights dancing across the sky. The lights were so bright he could barely see the stars twinkling above. To his amazement, he noticed he was the only tree that was awake.

Just then a band of at least a thousand angels flew overhead. Some were singing at the tops of their voices, while others fluttered around their friends, chirping in excitement. "Have you heard the news?"

The little tree could barely make out the shapes of the angels above him.

I wonder what news they are talking about? the little tree thought.

He listened hard, but just couldn't make out the words they were singing. As he watched, he noticed that one little girl angel was not flying as fast as the others. She was going so slowly, and was now trailing behind the others.

"Hello!" he called. "Hello, little angel! Can you hear me?"

"Who's calling me?" sang the little angel as she began flying closer to the earth.

"It's me; I'm over here between all the Douglas fir trees."

The little angel flew closer and closer to the earth, and then, just as wisps of Douglas fir pine needles brushed against her face, she saw the little tree.

"What kind of tree are you?" she asked. "You sure are different from the Douglas firs."

"I'm a pine tree."

"You are?" asked the puzzled little angel. "Are you sure? I mean, I have been learning all about pine trees at angel school, and you don't look like a ponderosa pine or a white pine or even a limber pine ."

"I'm not sure what kind of pine tree I am. All the Douglas firs tease me and say I'm a freak because my cones grow upwards at the tips of my branches."

The little angel flew closer to have a good look at the odd little cones.

"Hmmm," she muttered. "You are right. But your cones remind me of candles. Yes, that's what they remind me of, candles."

"What's a candle?"

"Well, it's something that lights up the dark. It is made of wax, and it has a wick in the centre, and it burns—"

The little tree shuddered in horror. "Fire," he said softly, so as not to wake any of the tall firs around him. "I don't want to be like a fire. The Douglas fir trees say that all the trees and animals living in the forest hate fire because it can destroy them." He gave another shudder.

"Candles are not mean and nasty," said the little angel hastily. "Candles are the lights that the Creator can see from heaven when he looks down to check on all the people at night. He likes candles."

"Oh," said the little tree, somewhat reassured. "Anyway, I don't think that my cones burn like candles, because if they did, I would have been burnt by now."

The angel giggled and said, "I guess you're right. Why aren't you sleeping? It is the middle of winter, you know."

The little pine had almost forgotten why he had called the baby angel.

"I was wondering why all the angels are so excited. They are all singing, and even the aurora borealis is showing off tonight. What's happening?"

"Oh, haven't you heard? We are here to tell everyone about the Baby."

"Baby? Which baby?"

"The Baby who is going to show all people how important it is to love everyone and everything in creation. We are all going to see him now," said the little angel happily.

"May I go too?" asked the tree.

The little angel shook her head and said, "You don't have any wings, and it is a very long way."

"How will I welcome the new Baby?" asked the tree.

"I could give him a message. What would you like me to tell him?"

"Would you please tell him, um, could you please tell him, um..." The tree sighed. "I don't know why he would want to hear from me. He wouldn't want to hear from a tree with funny, stick-up pinecones," he said sadly.

"Sure he would! What do you think you would like someone to say to you, on the day you were born?"

"I would like them to say that they were glad that I was here, and that they love me and they will take care of me, until I am big and can take care of myself."

"That's just what I will tell him."

"Will you tell me all about it when you come back?" asked the little tree.

"I won't be able to go back to sleep until I hear all about him."

"I'll come and tell you all about it," said the little angel as she flew after the other angels, her little wings beating as fast as they could as she tried to catch up to them.

Deep in the cold forest, the little tree waited and waited through the long, wintry night. Slowly the bright lights of the aurora borealis began to fade, and the night grew darker and darker. A wolf began to howl, and was soon joined in his song by the rest of the members of his pack. The little tree's needles trembled; the sound of the howling in the forest made him wish the other trees were awake. He was very afraid! Even the owls on their silent wings frightened him when they peered at him with their large, golden eyes.

After what seemed to be a very long time of being too scared to sleep, the tree heard the little angel calling him.

"Pine tree, young pine tree, where are you?'

"I'm here!"

"Yes, there you are!" she exclaimed. "I see you have managed to stay awake."

"Did you tell him, did you tell him?" asked the tree impatiently.

"Of course I told him."

"What did he say?"

"He didn't say anything, 'cause he is so new he hasn't learned to talk yet."

"Ohhh," said the little tree sadly.

"I have a message from his mother; she said to tell you that he was very happy to hear from you, and that you are a very special tree."

"I am?"

"Yes, you are. Then she said you were to stretch out your branches as long as possible and point your cones up towards the evening star."

"Why would I do that?" asked the puzzled little tree.

"Try it and let's see what happens," she replied.

Slowly the little tree stretched out its branches as far as they could reach.

Then he made the pinecones, which grew on the tips of his branches, reach up to the brightest star in the sky. They reached and reached and reached. Just when he felt they couldn't reach any further, something strange began to happen. At first it felt prickly, as if the tips of the cones had pins and needles in them. And then as the tree and the angel watched, the cones began to glow. A fuzzy, soft, yellowish light shone from each cone, and as they watched, the light grew clearer and brighter, until all the Douglas firs could be seen standing right next to the little pine tree.

The angel gasped and said, "You are so beautiful! You are the most beautiful tree in the forest on such a cold winter's night!"

The owl hooted in astonishment at the sight of the tree's glowing cones. A jackrabbit popped out of his burrow to take a closer look at the tree.

The little tree was too surprised to talk; all he could do was nod gently.

"My cones are so beautiful, and they aren't burning! I can't possibly hurt anything, can I?" the tree finally blurted out.

"No, you couldn't burn anything," agreed the angel. "You are a Candle Tree."

"Will they always be like this?" asked the tree, as he wiggled one of the cones.

"Oh, no! The Baby's mother said only one Candle Tree would be chosen to glow on the anniversary of her Baby's birth. Every year it would be a different Candle Tree in a different forest."

"How will we know which tree it will be?"

"You won't. It will be a secret until the Baby's birthday."

Nathaniel leaned back in his chair, his eyes bright with surprise and said, "Mom, do you mean I am representing that tree in the Nativity play?"

"Yes, Nathaniel, you are representing the little tree who sent a message of welcome to the special Baby so long ago."

"I think I like being a tree after all, Mom." With that, Nathaniel finished his hot chocolate and went to play.

After dinner, the Jon family walked over to the church hall where the Nativity play was to take place. Mother helped Nathaniel into his costume, and then took a small battery out of her purse. She tucked it into a small pocket in the branch near his fingertips. Nathaniel had never noticed the pocket before. "What's that, Mom?" he asked.

"It's a surprise that your dad and I have made for you. When it is your turn—"

"Where is the Candle Tree?" called Mrs. King, the Sunday school teacher.

"Here I am, Mrs. King." Nathaniel, in his tree costume, swayed onto the stage.

"Oh, dear, I didn't have time to tell him what to do," Mother said to her husband.

Father rushed after Nathaniel and whispered in his ear, "Remember to push the button when you are at the Baby's crib, son."

Nathaniel nodded.

The curtain rose, and the story of the Nativity began to unfold before the parents and families of each child. Eventually it was time for all the children in the play to make their way to the Baby's crib to offer their gift.

The three wise men presented the Baby's family with their gifts of gold, myrrh, and frankincense first. Each wise man laid his gift next to the crib.

The other members followed, until finally it was the Candle Tree's turn. Slowly, Nathaniel shuffled over to the crib and then pressed the button his parents had shown him. To his amazement, the tips of his cones began to shine.

"Oh, my," he said softly, beaming from ear to ear. "It's just like the little Candle Tree in the forest."

The audience gasped in amazement, and then began to clap.

"Wow!" said Mrs. King, "What a magnificent gift! Well done, Nathaniel. Perhaps the other children don't know that when the Candle Tree glows in the forest on Christmas Eve, the creatures of the forest come out of their winter dens so that they, too, can celebrate this special night."

At precisely midnight that Christmas Eve, an old pine tree growing in a forest in Northern British Columbia was woken by a strange feeling in the tips of her branches. When she opened her eyes, she was amazed to see that her cones were glowing. She was so surprised she called out to the trees around her. "Wake up, everyone!" Her husky voice carried in the breeze.

Slowly the other trees, the Douglas firs and the white pines, opened their eyes. The glowing pinecones on the old tree lit up the woods. At first the trees stood silently, and then they began to talk. It was the chattering of the white pines and the Douglas firs that woke the animals from their winter nap. A fox pushed the snow away from the front of his den and peered out into the glowing light of the forest. Squirrels crowded the openings to their nests in the hollows of some of the trees. They all stared in awe at the old Candle Tree.

Finally a limber pine said, "So, the legend of the Secret of the Candle Tree is true. See how beautiful she has become! It will always remind us of the Baby who came to make this world a better place to live in." All the other trees nodded their heads and swayed in the glow. As the light faded from the old Candle Tree's cones, the rest of the trees fell into a deep sleep again. The animals, whispering quietly among themselves, returned to their warm beds and were soon sound asleep. And all was quiet in the forest again.`

Printed in the United States
By Bookmasters